MR. MEN
LITTLE MISS

Easter Bunny

Roger Hargreaves

Original concept by
Roger Hargreaves

Written and illustrated by
Adam Hargreaves

It was a beautiful spring day and Little Miss Tiny was enjoying a walk in the countryside.

The flowers were out in bloom.
The lambs were skipping around the meadow.
The birds were building their nests in the trees.
And Easter was nearly here.

As Little Miss Tiny walked along, she wondered what sort of egg the Easter Bunny would bring her this year.

Suddenly, she was bowled over by someone running at great speed up the lane.

Well, it wasn't really running. It was more like high-speed hopping.

The figure shot past
Little Miss Tiny in a blur,
but even so, she recognised
who it was.

Or who she thought it was.

The Easter Bunny!

Little Miss Tiny raced into the woods after the Easter Bunny, but she lost sight of him.

However, she did find a small door in amongst the roots of a giant oak tree.

A small round bright yellow door.

The door to a rabbit burrow, possibly?

Maybe, thought Little Miss Tiny, this was where the Easter Bunny lived.

Little Miss Tiny circled round the tree and found a tiny round window on the other side. She peered in.

And there, pacing backwards and forwards, was the Easter Bunny. A very flustered Easter Bunny.

Little Miss Tiny went back round to the front door and knocked. After a short wait the door opened.

"Yes?" said the Easter Bunny.

"You seem to be in a spot of trouble and I wondered if I could help?" offered Little Miss Tiny.

"Well, mmm, yes, yes, forgot to set my alarm clock, way behind, so much to do, yes, yes, maybe you can help. Follow me!" blurted out the Easter Bunny.

With which the Easter Bunny plunged down a passageway and Little Miss Tiny raced after him.

It twisted and turned deeper underground until it opened out into an enormous burrow …

An enormous burrow full of whirring clanking machinery.

It was the Easter Bunny's Easter egg factory!

And busily working away were all the Easter Bunny's little helpers.

His Easter chicks.

They were mixing and blending and flavouring and colouring chocolate.

And moulding and shaping and wrapping and packaging eggs. Chirping happily as they worked.

Little Miss Tiny was amazed.

"Now, we have all sorts of Easter eggs for all sorts of people and we need to create the right egg for the right person," explained the Easter Bunny.

The two of them sat down and designed the best Easter egg for each person on the Easter Bunny's list.

It was a very long list!

Once they had finally finished the Easter Bunny said, "Now we'd better help the chicks load up my basket."

"How are we going to fit all these Easter eggs into one basket?" asked Little Miss Tiny.

"All will be revealed in a moment," smiled the Easter Bunny.

The Easter Bunny then led Little Miss Tiny to a lift, which took them to a branch high up in the oak tree where there was an enormous motorised flying wicker basket.

"Blimey," said Little Miss Tiny in awe.

"I know!" grinned the Easter Bunny with pride.

With the help of the Easter chicks, they loaded the eggs on board.

"Would you like to deliver the eggs with me?" asked the Easter Bunny.

Little Miss Tiny couldn't think of anything she would like to do more.

The Easter Bunny launched the basket into the air as the sun set and they sped off across the night sky, delivering the Easter eggs as they went.

And I guess the big question is, did the Easter Bunny and Little Miss Tiny find the right egg for the right person?

Let's find out!

Mr Silly woke up and found his Easter Egg.

A square one!

A square egg in
a round box.

Mr Greedy woke up to
an enormous egg.

Filled with caramel.

Which, of course, he ate for breakfast!

Little Miss Splendid's egg came in a splendidly ornate case.

Little Miss Dotty's egg was covered in spots.

Little Miss Late's had a Christmas wrapper, because she was always late opening it.

Easter at Christmas!

Mr Busy's Easter egg didn't come in a box, or wrapped in foil, to save time in his very busy day.

Easter on the run.

And Mr Lazy's egg came on a tray.

Easter in bed!

Little Miss Sunshine's egg had chocolate butterflies in it. Little Miss Magic's had a rabbit and Mr Mean's contained chocolate coins, which he wished were real.

Little Miss Lucky's was filled with real gold coins!
Mr Funny's had a joke inside and Little Miss Scary's
contained a surprise!

Mr Slow had a frozen egg,
so that it didn't melt before
he got it unwrapped.

Little Miss Shy had a big egg.

Big enough to hide her blushes.